ROGER PRICE'S

THE

TOMORROW
PEOPLE

THE MAN WHO
SOLD THE WORLD

Rebecca Levene & David Derbyshire

The Tomorrow People:
The Man Who Sold the World
Written by Rebecca Levene
& David Derbyshire
Published in 2025 by
Oak Tree Books
oaktreebooks.uk

in association with
Chinbeard Books

Editor: Paul Simpson
Commissioning/Sub-Editor: Barnaby Eaton-Jones

Cover artwork: Robert Hammond
Layout and Typesetting: Joe Larkins

Rebecca Levene &
David Derbyshire

The Tomorrow People

in

THE MAN WHO
SOLD THE WORLD

A Chinbeard Books / Oak Tree Books Original

Contents

To Nicholas Young, Elizabeth Adare
and Peter Vaughan-Clarke.

The Tomorrow People

Their names are John Dixon, Stephen Jameson and Elizabeth M'Bondo. They seem to be just ordinary kids. A bit quieter than most, perhaps. They are not from a distant future, they live on Earth, here and now. They are The Tomorrow People, forerunners of a new race, *homo superior* or even *homo novus*, which is why they are reasonably young. They are nature's response to man's aggression: a new species, wiser and more peace-loving than *homo sapiens*, for they cannot kill. They have gained remarkable powers: they can talk to each other by thought waves – telepathy. They can influence objects in the same way – telekinesis or psychokinesis. And they can think themselves from place to place as well – teleportation, but they call it jaunting. They wear a jaunting belt to help them with the complex details of navigation (and to ensure they don't end up underwater, or inside a brick wall) but they don't need it for short jaunts when they know where they are going and can picture it in their minds.

Until more of their race evolve, or "break out" as they call it, these four have intergalactic responsibility for the future of planet Earth, under the guidance of the Galactic Federation, based aboard their impossibly huge space-station, known colloquially as the Trig. The Galactic Federation have gifted the Tomorrow People a biotronic living computer known as TIM (Technobiologically Informed Mentor), to help and guide them. TIM has been installed in a secret laboratory where, when they are not in their normal homes, the Tomorrow People can meet, work, play and even sleep and eat. The Lab itself was built by John, underneath an old disused London Underground station, where no one ever goes.

The Tomorrow People also have friends that aren't part of their new evolution, two very ordinary humans called Ginge and Chris who help the Tomorrow People in whatever purely human way they can.

With thanks to Roger Price and Brian Finch.

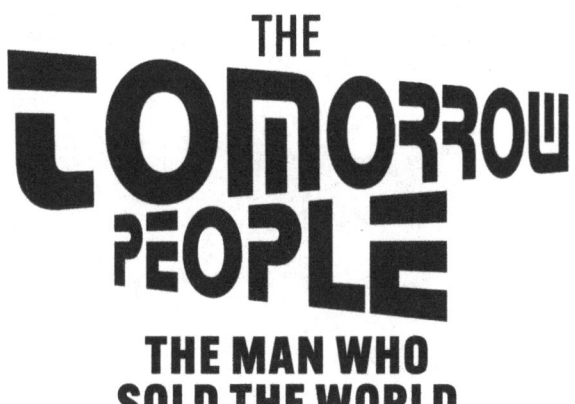

THE

TOMORROW PEOPLE

THE MAN WHO
SOLD THE WORLD

1: Time

She was old beyond imagination. She was born long before the first aeroplanes soared through the clouds of the planet Earth, before the first ships explored the oceans, before the first human farmers gathered seeds under the Mesopotamian sky.

Every year of every millennium that she had lurked in the darkness of her world she had grown in size and in strength. Her brain – if you could call the ganglia that ran like veins through her tissues a brain – had developed extraordinary powers.

There had been no others like her, but she had no concept of loneliness. There was only her and the world around her. The strange, alien creatures that flitted in and out of her sphere of influence were too primitive for conversation and good only for food. Occasionally, perhaps once every decade, there came along a many-limbed animal intelligent enough to act as a host for her young, but most of those offspring died. When they did, she felt nothing. She consumed their bodies and continued her existence eating, resting and watching.

Then, not very long ago, he had made contact. His was a voice in the darkness, a light in the void. And she had welcomed him and reached out to him over the impossible distance to his strange world, discovering the pleasure of companionship. She had learned how to communicate thoughts and make herself understood.

Now their plans had come to fruition, and she was finally in his world. And what a world it was. The air was rich with thoughts and sounds and chemicals and noise, and the human lifeforms, with their tiny lives and shallow ambitions, were so wonderfully vulnerable and so marvellously ripe for exploitation.

She had known the moment he made contact that the humans would be the perfect hosts for her babies. And this time, she would produce millions and millions. In their new form, they would dominate this world and spread among the stars. Soon. Very soon.

Sixty yards below the litter-strewn streets of London in a disused Underground station, John was running out of time.

This was stupid, he thought, he was more than capable of getting this done. On paper it had looked easy, but the movement was so complicated and so unnatural that his fingers just didn't seem able to find their way. He checked the instructions again.

The voice of TIM boomed above his head. 'John, do you require assistance?'

'I'm fine, TIM, really. I just need to find the right gap.' He tried again and gave up. 'Blast it. It should be straightforward. I'm not an idiot. So why on Earth can't I manage to tie a bow tie?'

'Bow ties are notoriously difficult. I can always create a clip-on one for you.' Was it John's imagination, or did he detect amusement in TIM's voice?

It was possible, of course. TIM was not an ordinary machine. He was a biotronic computer capable of original thought and built into the very structure of the Lab. His consciousness was housed in the silver hemispheres fixed to the ceiling and in the translucent biofluid connectors, the tubes containing a living liquid that pulsed and shimmered, casting multi-coloured patterns across the room.

'Thank you, TIM, but I'm more than able to do this without your help.'

He tried again, and this time, miraculously, the tie began to take shape. *Finally*. He stepped back and scrutinised the effect in the mirror. That wasn't too bad at all.

The others would be back soon and he was eager to be on his way before they arrived. He picked up his dinner jacket and was giving his hair one last comb when, to his dismay, he saw the lights on the teleportation platform begin to glow and two figures materialised in front of him: Elizabeth M'Bondo and Stephen Jameson. Both were clutching shopping bags.

'I don't think I'll ever get used to that,' Elizabeth said, stepping down from the platform.

'Course you will,' Stephen said. 'Jaunting gets easier over time. And it's a lot quicker than getting the train.'

It had been just eight weeks since Elizabeth discovered she was a Tomorrow Person. She was still adjusting to her newly emerged powers and John was impressed with how well she was coping.

As the group's leader, it was his job to take care of the younger Tomorrow People, and he took it as seriously as he took most things.

'You've spruced up rather well, John.' Elizabeth eyed his dinner jacket with a smile. 'Going on a date?'

John tutted. 'There's nothing wrong with looking respectable. If you must know, I'm meeting an eminent scientist for dinner.'

'She wouldn't be a lady scientist by any chance, would she?' Stephen asked.

'Really, Stephen, some of us have more than one thing on our mind. As it happens, Dr Mary Hungerford is a highly respected neurologist and an expert in the unchannelled mental potential of Saps.' Very keen to change the subject, he added, 'Good shop?'

'Excellent,' Elizabeth said. 'I needed some new clothes for school. If I'm going to be sleeping here from time to time, I can't keep turning up in the same outfit every day.'

'And I've been saving up for this,' Stephen said, rummaging in a bag. He triumphantly held up a box with a spiral graphic on one side. 'They'd sold out in Oxford Street, which is why we had to go all the way to Manchester. It's a Theta Mindstone.'

John frowned. 'A what?'

'Come on, John, you must have been living under a rock for the last six months if you've not heard of Mindstones. They're massive.'

'Well, they appear to have passed me by. What on Earth is a Theta Mindstone? A game?'

'No. They're a kind of aid for meditation,' Stephen explained. 'They're incredible. I tried one last week at school. They're touch sensitive and they respond to your brain patterns with light and sounds and not just that. You can make them do lots of amazing stuff.'

'I'm surprised you've not heard of them,' Elizabeth said. 'Half the kids in my class have got them and the adverts are everywhere – Elliot Jackson makes them.'

Elliot Jackson was someone John had heard of: one of the UK's leading philanthropists and entrepreneurs. A hippie in the nineteen sixties, he'd turned his hand to business in the last few years with remarkable success.

Stephen looked like he was about to burst with enthusiasm. 'Jackson keeps creating incredible stuff; he's nearly as good an inventor as you, John. He makes a fortune and then gives almost all of it away to charity. The stuff he comes up with, well, it really is mind blowing.'

'I didn't realise you were such a big fan of business

6

ventures, Stephen. I can never get you interested in *my* work.'

'No disrespect, John, but Jackson's not your typical inventor.' Stephen looked almost sheepish. 'I got his autobiography today too.' He took out a hardback from his bag. The cover was a photograph of a man with a pony tail and round glasses wearing a green and pink tie-dye T-shirt. The book's title, *Tune In, Get On!,* was emblazoned across the cover in shocking pink.

'He's certainly got an eye for publicity,' John said drily. 'And if you're such a fan of his, you'll no doubt be pleased to hear that the scientist I'm meeting this evening works for one of his institutes.'

'No way.' Stephen looked genuinely impressed. 'Hey, John, you couldn't fix me up with a tour, could you? And then maybe I could get to meet him.'

TIM interrupted. 'John, you won't be meeting anyone tonight unless you leave now. I made the reservation at Simpsons for six thirty at your request, and you are now running one minute late.'

'Simpsons, eh? Very swanky. Be good,' Elizabeth said with a grin.

'And make sure you're home by ten thirty,' Stephen added. 'We don't want you gallivanting around London late at night with your lady friend.'

'Honestly, you're both so childish,' John muttered as he stepped on to the jaunting pad and vanished.

Elliot Jackson lent back in his desk chair and pushed himself round in circles with his feet until he was dizzy. Today had been one of those great days, the sort that would make an entire chapter in his next autobiography. Not that he was going to write another autobiography, of course, certainly not one that anyone would be reading. But still.

He had stayed the previous night at his flat in Mayfair and breakfasted early with the Prime Minister, appeared on BBC Radio Four's *Today* programme for a jokey interview with the host John Timpson and then toured the newly opened Theta Mindstone store in Regent's Street for the press. The store was magnificent. It occupied the entire ground floor of a grand Georgian building and was unlike any shop London had seen before, in that it sold just one product. After lunch he had flown by helicopter back here to the Elliot Jackson Institute.

He buzzed through to his PA. 'Can you get me Mary Hungerford please, Edith?' His voice, like so much of his carefully cultivated image, was warm and matey, a blend of mid-Atlantic with just a hint of cockney to highlight his common touch.

'Sorry, Elliot, she's left early.'

That's right, he thought. She'd told him yesterday. She was off on a date with some mysterious inventor she wanted to recruit to the team. He smiled indulgently. Let her have her fun. She worked hard enough.

Yes, today had been a great day. And tomorrow would be better. He picked up a copy of his autobiography and browsed through the well-thumbed pages.

'Elliot.'

The voice, calm, gentle and soothing, filled the room. Like Jackson's, it had a faint mid-Atlantic tinge.

Jackson rose, walked to the centre of his office and sat down at a mahogany table shaped like a seashell. The table was almost entirely filled with a gigantic white pebble, some six feet long, which had started to pulse yellow and green.

'I'm here,' he said.

'Just checking in for an update,' the voice said.

'Man, things could not be better. I spoke with the boys at the store and we're well on the way.

They reckon we're on course to have total market saturation in one week.'

'That's quicker than you thought.'

Jackson grinned. 'I know. People are literally freaking out over the stones. It's unreal. We can't shift them fast enough. You okay to keep the supply up?"

'Don't worry about me, Elliot. I'm just delighted that they're selling so well. What about the first activations?'

'Very soon – everything's in place,' Jackson said. And he sat back in the chair with a benign-looking smile.

2: Fill Your Heart

The meal was going well. John was fond of Elizabeth and Stephen, even when they were being as insufferable as they'd been earlier, but it was nice to get away and spend time with a fellow scientist. And he had to admit, Mary was rather more presentable than most of the scientists John had come across, with long, red hair and crystalline green eyes shining behind fashionable glasses.

The restaurant was dimly lit, with dark wooden panelling, candles on all the tables, and sharply pressed white linen napkins. John used his to dab a fleck of Diane sauce from his lip.

'I must say, this is an awfully nice place you've chosen,' Mary said, tucking into her own lobster thermidor, which he couldn't help thinking was going to set him back a bob or two.

'It's quiet, which is the main thing,' John told

her. 'I'm very keen to hear about your latest research and this seems to be one of the few restaurants left that doesn't deafen its customers with music'.

'Oh, oh yes,' Mary said, looking oddly crestfallen. For a moment John felt a pang of disappointment. That was odd. He had been enjoying the meal and the company and the emotion was unexpected. He brushed the feeling aside as Mary continued. 'Well, for the last few months it's been nothing but Theta Mindstones for me. You know about them, don't you?'

'I hear they're all the rage.'

'They're a groundbreaking innovation, absolutely groundbreaking!' She leaned forward in her enthusiasm, her lobster temporarily forgotten. 'If they live up to our expectations, they could represent a transformation in human consciousness. It could mean the end of war.'

John found himself leaning forward and smiling, swept up by an almost overpowering wave of enthusiasm, which was peculiar, because he was usually a person who kept his cool. It was almost as if he was mirroring Mary's own mood, or rather, that she was *broadcasting* her feelings to him, like a TP. She wasn't, of course, he would have sensed that the moment they had met at that conference a few weeks ago. But could she have a little telepathic talent herself? Too little and too late for her to become a TP, of course, but intriguing, nonetheless.

Seeing John's interested expression, Mary said, 'The preliminary results have been extraordinary. You won't believe how this will change people.'

'For the better, I hope,' John said, laughing.

'Oh, it's very easy to be cynical. But Mr Jackson is an idealist – he genuinely believes he can guide the future of humanity. Help everyone become the best versions of themselves.'

'That's rather grandiose, don't you think?'

'There's nothing grandiose about wanting the best for the human race. And you're a fine one to talk. What about your own paper on the neural basis for unlocking the potential of the human brain? You were sixteen when you wrote that, weren't you? Quite the teenage prodigy.'

'Fifteen,' he corrected, flattered that she knew so much about him. He'd been right: their research interests really did intersect.

They chatted about recent advances in silicon technology, and how long before artificial intelligence became a reality. Of course, John wasn't able to tell her that it already had – he had TIM as evidence – but he enjoyed the conversation all the same. And if she really was a latent telepath, it would explain why he felt himself so drawn to her. Well, that and his admiration for her work, of course.

As they rose to leave, she said, 'I've enjoyed our conversation awfully much. And I was wondering… since you seem unconvinced about Mr Jackson's plans, how would you feel about a visit to our labs in Hertfordshire? Chaperoned by me, of course.' Her eyes dropped from his as she said it, as if she was a little embarrassed by the invitation.

'I'd like it very much!' John said. 'There's still so much to talk about. We haven't even touched on neural imaging yet…'

In the Lab, Elizabeth had hung up her new clothes in her locker. 'I'm off,' she said, 'I've got a pile of marking at home.'

'I thought the point of being an art teacher was that you didn't have to do any marking?' Stephen said.

'Thank you very much. I know you think that doing teacher training is a doddle, but I take my job extremely seriously. And if you must know, I've got until the end of the week to get through the entire fifth year's CSE coursework. You okay to entertain yourself?'

'Honestly, Elizabeth, I'm not a child. You sometimes seem to forget we're not at school anymore.' His voice was snappier than he had intended, and Elizabeth looked wounded.

'I don't think that's fair, Stephen. I think *you* forget that it's only been eight weeks since I broke out. And eight weeks ago, you *were* just another pupil in my class. '

'Oh, thanks.'

'You know what I mean, don't be so silly.'

Stephen could feel the irritation continue to froth up inside him, like the boiling pans of strawberry jam his mother used to make. 'It's not been easy, you know. Every day I have to go into that school and pretend to be just another Sap. I feel like I'm walking around with both my hands tied behind my back and with sticking plaster over my mouth. And I have to pretend that I don't know you outside of school, too. I can't even stick up for you properly.'

'What do you mean "stick up for me"?'

'When the other kids say things, I have to sit there and ignore it.'

'What exactly are they saying?'

'Things. The stupid sort of things that kids say about teachers, especially the young student teachers. They already think I've got a thing for you. They tease me all the time. You have no idea how difficult it is.'

Elizabeth bristled. 'Well, I'm sorry you don't feel able to defend me. I thought better of you than that, Stephen. But I'm perfectly capable of fighting my own battles. And for goodness' sake, tidy this place up before John gets back. It's like a bomb's hit it.'

She vanished before he could reply. It's not fair, he thought. Elizabeth was actually only three years older than him, but sometimes she acted more like his mother than his own mum.

He was used to living a double life, of course. It was more than a year since he had broken out and been discovered by John – along with Carol and Kenny, who had since gone off to work with the Galactic Federation. His mum and dad knew about his special powers, but they were among only a handful of people who did. And even his mum and dad couldn't possibly understand the responsibility that came from being a TP.

The annoyance in his bones was still there, and he felt on edge, as if he'd eaten too much sugar, or spent too long stuck inside on a sunny day. What he needed was a way to let off steam, and the Theta Mindstone was the ideal distraction. He took the stone to the sleeping area off the Lab and made himself comfortable on the bed.

The stone was the size of a large potato and made from a kind of soft plastic that yielded to his squeeze. It was a sterile white, but the moment Stephen picked it up, its colour shifted to a faint purple. The longer he held it, the deeper the colour became, and it started to pulse in response to his heartbeat and emit a soothing hum.

Stephen lay back, held the stone between the palms of his hands and concentrated. The secret was to get his brainwave patterns relaxed. He breathed deeply and let his mind empty. The stone's purple light grew brighter and then began to change, fluidly moving from purple to red, then blue, then green. He could feel the surface rippling gently in his hands and begin to get warmer.

The sound became more tuneful – not quite music, but musical. He focused on the sound and discovered he could change the notes by relaxing further. The calmer he felt, the more melodic the sound became.

He shifted his weight, and his foot knocked the packaging to the floor. The noise distracted him and the sound from the stone changed to a grating metallic buzz.

He tried hard to regain his focus, and this time sensed a surge of euphoria which filled his body from his toes up through his chest and into his head.

The waves grew more powerful, until he felt he was floating on a sea, staring up at the night sky. He had never experienced anything so calming or pleasurable. There was something warm and irresistible. He felt like he was being cocooned with love, an overpowering sensation of being wanted and needed. And the more he relaxed, the more his mind emptied, the greater the feeling of love. Everything was perfect, everything was calm. He was at one with the universe and he was wanted and needed.

He struggled to keep his eyes open for a few minutes, but then gave in…

'Stephen, are you alright?' It was Elizabeth's voice. She sounded anxious.

Stephen was half asleep. He blinked his eyes. 'What?'

'Are you okay?'

'Of course. I dozed off.'

'We were extremely anxious about you, Stephen,' TIM said. 'I've been attempting to wake you for five minutes with no success. I contacted Elizabeth. I thought it best not to disturb John.'

'Relax, the pair of you, I was just napping.'

Elizabeth's eyes flashed dangerously. 'Napping? You were barely conscious.'

Stephen's head was still groggy. The sense of perfection was ebbing away, but he still felt relaxed. 'I was using the stone. It was incredible! It felt like I was, well, floating in heaven. Really. I must have dropped off, I suppose. How long was I asleep, TIM?'

'Nearly three hours, Stephen.'

'Blimey. But really, there's no need to get all worked up, Elizabeth.'

'Worked up? I was worried sick. TIM thought you were in a coma. And look at the state of this

19

place! I asked you to tidy up and you've done nothing but lie there. It's all very well you achieving Nirvana, but I'm having to live in this muck. Look, there's even silverfish in here.'

She pointed. Two silvery shapes were sliding across the floor towards the bed. Stephen hurriedly lifted his feet onto the bed with a feeling of revulsion. He was still clutching the Theta Mindstone at the time he saw the creatures. It let out a squeal, like the sound of a tom cat fighting in a nighttime garden.

'Yuk, I can't bear silverfish,' Stephen said. 'They're disgusting.'

'Honestly, they're only insects, don't make such a fuss.'

'Elizabeth is perfectly right, Stephen, Silverfish are harmless and extremely useful,' TIM said. 'They feed on debris such as dead insects and food waste. In fact, they are such efficient housekeepers, that the nanite robots that keep my own biological systems clear are designed on similar principles.'

Stephen still didn't look convinced.

'Just clean up this place,' Elizabeth said as she turned on her heel and left.

'She's worse than my mum,' he said to no one in particular. He put down the stone, which had stopped squealing, and opened the cleaning cupboard to retrieve the broom. 'TIM, what's the best way to get rid of silverfish?'

'The best way is to keep the room clean and tidy in the first place, Stephen,' said TIM.

'That's a fat lot of help,' Stephen muttered as he set to work.

Elizabeth went to her own home for the night after the conversation with Stephen. Well, it had been more of an argument, if she was honest with herself. And she didn't relish the prospect of sleeping in an alcove next to him for the night, stewing over what had been said. She tossed and turned in her own bed, instead. She hated being at odds with people, but Stephen really was behaving unreasonably. It seemed out of character, but then how well did she really know him?

It was Saturday the next day, which meant no school. So, she jaunted over to the Lab; mainly to find out how John's date had gone.

When she arrived, with the strange, light-headed sensation jaunting always brought, it was to find him working on TIM. Stephen was lying on his bed, even though it was already 10 o'clock. He was playing with that silly stone again.

'Hello, Elizabeth,' John said, looking up from his work. 'Everything all right? You look like you rolled out of the wrong side of bed this morning.'

'I had a bit of a restless night,' she admitted. 'But I'm much more interested in *your* night, John. How did the date go? Sorry, I meant your extremely professional meeting with an eminent scientist.'

John rolled his eyes. 'It went very well, thank you. In fact, I'll be seeing her again in a few days. She's invited me for a tour of Jackson's Institute.'

Stephen had seemed to be in a world of his own, but now he sat up, face alight with interest. 'Really? You lucky so-and-so. I'd give anything for a chance to look inside that place. You might even get to meet Elliot Jackson himself!'

'Actually, Stephen, I thought you might like to come with me. I'm sure Mary wouldn't mind, and she's said that she's planning to introduce me to Jackson. I'll explain that you're a protégé of mine.'

Honestly, John really was hopeless sometimes. 'Are you certain about that?' Elizabeth asked. 'I think Mary might like to have you to herself.'

'Oh, the more the merrier, I'm sure.'

'Don't you go trying to change his mind,' Stephen said. 'This is the best thing that's happened to me all week! *I* get to meet Elliot Jackson. I can't believe it.'

'I wouldn't get your hopes too high,' Elizabeth told him. 'Idols tend to have feet of clay.'

John turned his attention back to his work. 'When I'm there, I might ask Mary's advice on boosting TIM's telepathic link. I've managed a thirty per cent improvement, but I'm sure it could go higher. I won't tell her exactly what it is, of course. But she seemed to know her way around a circuit board and I'm sure she'd have some useful insights. It is very nice to have someone to talk to who really understands my work.'

Elizabeth was sure John didn't mean it to sting, but it did. She knew that she lacked the technical know-how of John, or even Stephen. She was a trainee art teacher, for heaven's sake! She sometimes wondered if her developing her TP powers had been some kind of mistake. It was hard to imagine she'd be as much use to the Galactic Trig as Carol or Kenny seemed to be.

'Stephen,' John said, 'Could you pass me that hammer please? The one on the shelf. I don't want to let go of this wire.'

Stephen sighed, as if what John had asked him was a terrible imposition. After his brief flash of interest when Elliot Jackson had been mentioned, he'd gone back to brooding over his Theta Mindstone. Now he waved his hand negligently, like a magician performing a spell, and Elizabeth felt the noiseless surge of his telekinetic powers. The hammer hovered in the air, then went flying off the shelf all on its own—

—heading straight for Elizabeth's head! He'd sent it off in completely the wrong direction. She managed to use her own telekinesis to bat it away just in time, and it clattered to the floor near John's feet.

John hadn't even looked up from his work, and Stephen hadn't noticed. He was absorbed in this Theta Mindstone again, which was glowing a rather violent orange. *Well*, Elizabeth thought, *I may not be the brainiest Tomorrow Person around, but at least I pay attention when it matters.* It wasn't a terribly comforting thought.

3: Come and Buy My Toys

'It's like something out of a Hammer Horror movie,'
Stephen said as he and John walked along the gravel
driveway towards Happledon Grange, the home of
the Elliot Jackson Institute.

Even from this distance, Stephen could see that
the roof was adorned with fairy-tale spires and gothic
turrets, and that the ivy-clad walls were topped with
castellations. And there were people standing on the
roof.

At John's insistence, they had jaunted to a
secluded copse in the grounds; half a mile from the
front door.

'Can't we just jaunt to the reception?' Stephen
had complained.

'Now come on Stephen, that's not like you. You
enjoy a spot of exercise normally. And you know
full well that it's vital we keep our special powers

secret. If the Saps discover what we can do, we'd be rounded up and detained for experimentation.'

They walked on, past the squawking ducks and geese that meandered in groups at the side of the ornamental lake. Stephen had woken with a headache, and it seemed to be getting worse with every step he took towards the house. It was threatening to put a dampener on a day he had been looking forward to ever since John had invited him.

'Are you sure we'll get to meet Elliot Jackson?' he asked.

John smiled paternally. 'Dr Hungerford said she couldn't guarantee it, but she'd do her best. Just don't get your hopes raised too highly. Meeting your heroes can sometimes be a bit of a let down.'

'Don't be such a killjoy – you're as bad as Elizabeth. And are you sure it's okay that I'm coming along?'

'Why ever not? Dr Hungerford said the Institute is always happy to welcome visitors – it's part of their ethos to be transparent.'

'Okay, but I don't want to be a gooseberry,' he said with a grin.

'What on Earth do you mean?' John asked.

But before Stephen could answer, they heard a

scrunching of tyres on gravel and turned to see what looked like a converted electric milk float pulling to a stop behind them on the drive. The driver was dressed in black leathers and a baseball cap, and a similarly attired man was standing on the back of the vehicle. To Stephen's alarm, he appeared to have a rifle slung over his shoulder.

'Oi!' the guard shouted. 'What are you doing here? This is private land.'

'So much for a warm welcome,' Stephen muttered. John shushed him.

'I'm sorry, is there a problem?' he called to the man. 'We have an invitation to tour the facilities.' He pulled out a sheet of paper.

The man jumped down from the vehicle and stalked over to them with a suspicious glare. He kept one hand on his gun in the holster. Stephen noticed that he was wearing a patch with an Elliot Jackson Institute logo – it was the same spiral that was on the packaging of the Theta Mindstone.

'How did you get in? Where's your pass? You didn't come through the main gate?' The guard's voice was aggressive and loud. He held a walkie-talkie to his mouth and said, 'Red four here, two intruders found on the main driveway, holding them, require back up.'

His colleague stepped out of the vehicle. He too was armed and was pointing his rifle at John.

'John?' Stephen spoke into John's mind.

'Don't worry, Stephen,' said John silently. *'It's just a mistake. I'll handle it.'*

The first man stepped closer. He looked at the letter in John's hand but didn't take it. 'I said, how did you get in?'

'As I told you, it's all here in this letter. We got a lift and were dropped off miles from the gate by mistake. We thought it would be okay to just hop across the wall. I think this is a bit of an over-reaction.'

The guard looked at John and Stephen and finally took the letter. He scrutinised it for several minutes, then returned to the vehicle and spoke on his walkie-talkie.

When he came back, his manner had softened. 'Okay, you're clear to move on. Just next time, use the main gate.' He clambered back into the vehicle, and it drove off.

'That was odd,' John said as they walked on, looking a bit shaken. 'Why on Earth does Elliot Jackson need armed guards?'

Stephen shrugged. 'He's probably worried about industrial espionage. Jackson's doing some amazing stuff – and he wants to give it to the world for free. But if a rival stole it, well, they'd make a fortune.'

'Hmm.' John sounded unconvinced.

The front door was an imposing oak monstrosity that creaked open at John's push and revealed a light, airy reception. It reminded Stephen of a hotel at first, until his nostrils caught the incense in the air.

There were bean bags everywhere and dozens of people lounging around. Many were dressed in brightly coloured tie-dye shirts and kaftans, and most of the men had long hair and beards. Many were using Theta Mindstones, some sitting cross-legged with the stones held in in their laps, others lying on mats, clutching the stones to their chests.

A woman with black glasses and red straight hair smiled with recognition and came over to John. She was wearing a white lab coat with a spiral logo on the breast pocket. Stephen noticed her smile flicker briefly when she saw that John wasn't alone, but she instantly corrected herself and beamed at both of them.

'John, lovely to see you. I didn't realise you were bringing a…' She struggled for the right words, '…a young friend.'

Stephen sensed a powerful wave of disappointment. Surprised, he looked around at John, but it wasn't him. It seemed to be coming from the woman. She couldn't be a TP – otherwise she'd have heard Stephen and John talking telepathically a few minutes earlier. John had told them he thought she might be a latent telepath, and it seemed he was right.

'I didn't think you'd mind,' John said to her. 'This is Stephen. He's a pupil of a friend of mine and is extremely keen on science and your boss, Mr Jackson. Stephen, this is Dr Mary Hungerford.'

'Pleased to meet you,' Stephen said, sticking out his hand. He could see a look of disappointment return to Dr Hungerford's face, but John seemed oblivious.

'Follow me, both of you, and we'll get you signed in,' she said.

'We were a bit surprised to see the rather heavy-handed security outside,' John said as they filled in their passes. 'We had a bit of a rough reception.'

'I'm so sorry, they do get a bit over enthusiastic sometimes. That's the problem in hiring former military. But it's just a precaution. Industrial espionage is a big problem and Elliot is extremely protective. He can't bear the thought of some of that money being lost to rivals who'll use it for private gain.'

Stephen looked smugly at John. *'Told you so,'* he crowed silently in his head.

'Even so, the guns seem a little excessive,' John said to Dr Hungerford.

'Will we get to meet Elliot, Mary?' Stephen asked.

'If there's time. Let's show you the research facilities first.'

'Who are all these… people?' John waved around him.

'They're our guests. As well as being a research institute, we have around fifty volunteers who live here. It's a commune if you will, a chance for people to come and join in. Some work in the gardens, others prepare the food or clean. It's extremely popular.'

'And do they get paid to work here?' John asked.

Dr Hungerford looked surprised. 'The opposite. They pay for the privilege of joining the community. We have quite a waiting list.'

'How much do they pay?'

She looked suddenly defensive. 'I'm not sure. It's around £100 a week, I think.'

Stephen whistled. 'Blimey, that's not cheap.'

'It certainly isn't,' John said. 'And what about the guards? I can't imagine your zealous security people

31

are too delighted to have a lot of hippies in kaftans wandering around.'

'The main parkland is out of bounds to the guests, but we have plenty of private gardens where they can go. I think you'll find the system works very well.' She looked irritated at John's questions.

Careful, John, or you'll blow your chances, Stephen thought, but only to himself.

It took thirty minutes for Dr Hungerford to show John and Stephen around the laboratories, the research rooms and the gardens. Everywhere they went, Jackson's staff, all dressed in the same white lab coats, were silent and focused. Dr Hungerford explained the functions of each room – the library, the design studio, the marketing suite, the engineering lab – but Stephen noticed she was vague about the details of what exactly the staff were so busy working on. In every room, sitar music was playing from loudspeakers in the ceiling.

Once the tour was complete, she left them alone for a few minutes to make a phone call, before returning with a smile. Again, Stephen sensed an emotion – this time satisfaction.

Mary turned to him. 'Well now, Stephen, you'll be pleased to hear that we've been able to schedule a few minutes with Elliot himself.'

Stephen couldn't hide the wide grin on his face as they followed her up a flight of red-carpeted stairs and into a smart ante room outside a closed wooden door. There was music coming from the other side. No, not music: whale song.

The door opened into a large wood-panelled circular study with a cream carpet so thick, Stephen could feel his shoes dragging as he walked over it.

The whale song was coming out of two gigantic speakers in the ceiling. On one side of the room was a hanging chair, on the other, a shelf with a large Newton's Cradle with balls the size of footballs, and a hi-fi system with a record spinning on the turntable. Stephen didn't know much about hi-fis, but he could tell that this one was top of the range.

In the centre of the room was a table on which had been placed an out-sized Theta Mindstone. On the wall were copies of classic paintings – the Mona Lisa, the Great Wave and Michelangelo's creation of Adam. The scent of incense hung heavily in the room.

The stone dominated the office, and it took Stephen a few moments to notice the figure with a ponytail and beard in a green and pink tie-dye T-shirt behind it. Elliot Jackson said nothing but walked to the record player and lifted the stylus.

Stephen noticed he was wearing brown leather gloves.

'It's a real honour to meet you, sir,' Stephen said, his heart beating faster than normal.

'Hey, hey, no need for "sirs" here. Stephen, isn't it? Just call me Elliot. And you must be John. Mary's told me so much about you. You're the inventor, right?'

'I dabble a little,' John said, modestly.

'More than a little, I hear. We must arrange for you to have a chat with some of our main brains here. Fancy a job? It's a cool place to hang out and the bread ain't bad!'

'Thank you, Mr Jackson – Elliot – but I'm already fully employed.'

'Hmm. Hey, come and have a look at the nerve centre.' He beckoned them over to a large glass window behind the desk. It looked out over a cavernous factory floor below.

The floor was dominated by a conveyor belt that emerged from a hole in the centre of the room and circled outwards in a spiral, carrying Theta Mindstones through half a dozen machines. Stephen could only guess the function of the first few bits of equipment on the production line, but the last couple were clearly for packaging. The stones left the last machine in a cardboard box and were carried by the belt to a loading bay, where men gathered the boxes and arranged them on pallets.

'It's a Fibonacci sequence,' Stephen said suddenly. 'I mean the design of the conveyor built – it circles round and out and round like a shell. It's the same design on your logo. And in the swimming pool in your house in LA.' Then he blushed.

Jackson studied him for a second and then his face shifted into a big, warm grin. 'Very cool, Stephen. I can see you've read my book. Yes, the conveyor belt follows the Fibonacci sequence: the Golden Ratio. I designed it. If you're going to create something, why not make it as cool as you can, you know? Must admit, the Golden Ratio is a weakness of mine.' He walked over to the paintings on the wall. 'Look, Leonardo used it in the Mona Lisa, and Michelangelo in the Sistine Chapel.'

There was a pause and John jumped in. 'Do you mind me asking what this is?' He pointed to the gigantic stone.

'Sure. It's an early concept design – non-functional, of course. But, you know, I loved it so much I asked the guys on the factory floor to mock me one up as a piece of art. Do you like it?'

'Well, it's very modern,' John said.

Stephen was still watching the factory floor. He counted twenty people working around the conveyor belt. All were wearing grey leather jumpsuits. 'What's underneath the floor?' he asked. 'How are the stones actually made? It looks like they've already been manufactured when they drop on the conveyor belt.'

Jackson smiled more warmly than ever. 'Haven't you got the curious mind, young Stephen. But I'm afraid that's got to be a secret. I know of a dozen guys – bad guys – who would just love to discover how we create the Mindstones. But be reassured, they are made with a real labour of love. Now, it's been such a blast meeting you, but I've gotta move. Mary will make sure you get a little something special on your way out.'

'Excuse me, Elliot,' Stephen said, 'but would you mind signing this?' He scrambled in his backpack and pulled out a copy of Jackson's autobiography.

'Of course,' Jackson said. He pulled out a fountain pen, removed one glove, and scribbled something on the fly sheet.

Later, as they were waved off by Dr Hungerford and walked down the drive, John asked Stephen to show him what Jackson had written.

'*Imagine no possessions*,' John read out. 'Not bad, coming from a millionaire. And did you notice his watch? A Rolex. Must have cost him over a hundred pounds.'

'You really didn't like him, did you?'

'To be honest, Stephen, no, I didn't. I think there's something fundamentally phony about him.'

Stephen felt a stirring of rage that was very unlike him. 'Unbelievable, John. He's a successful inventor, a philanthropist. I reckon this sounds like jealousy!'

Anger flashed across John's face, quickly replaced with a look which resembled disappointment. 'That's preposterous, Stephen. I can assure you that I am anything but jealous of Elliot Jackson. And I'm not sure he's such a great role model for you.'

They walked on in awkward silence.

In his office, Elliot Jackson took off his glasses and sat in his chair. He closed his eyes and focused on the stone in front of him. After a few moments, it began to glow.

'Elliot,' said a voice that seemed to come from all around the room. 'You were right. There is something intriguing about those two. Have they been given stones?'

'They were given them as they left, but it appears that that boy has possessed his own stone for some time and is a long way down the path already.

'Cool,' the voice said. 'Extremely cool. In that case, we won't have long to wait.'

4: Changes

'I'll tell you one thing,' John said. 'Elliot Jackson may be a phony, but his technology is extraordinary. I've not seen anything like it.'

He and the others were sitting on the sofas in the Lab drinking tea, provided by TIM. John had spent the last half hour studying the two stones that Dr Hungerford had handed them as a parting gift.

'Just look at these things,' he said. 'They're remarkable. I can't find any battery cover, so the power must be built in. I'd love to get one open to have a look at what's inside.'

'What did you make of the great man, Stephen? Did he live up to your expectations?' Elizabeth asked.

'Eh? Sorry, Elizabeth, I was miles away.'

John studied Stephen's face. There were purple rings around his eyes and his skin had a greenish-yellow tinge. 'Is that headache any better?'

'Not really, but it's fine.' Stephen stood, and suddenly clutched at the table.

'I think we'd better get TIM to take a look at you,' John said. 'TIM – run a level one medical diagnostic on Stephen, please. And meantime, let's get him on the bed.'

John and Elizabeth slipped his arms over their shoulders to support him as they led him to the sleeping bay. He sat for a moment on the mattress, his eyes bleary – and then slumped back, as if all the energy had suddenly drained out of him.

Elizabeth shook his shoulders. 'Stephen, wake up.' Her voice was panicky. And then she spoke to him without words. *'Stephen, Stephen, can you hear me?'* There was no reply. 'John, he's unconscious!' she said out loud again.

'I can find nothing wrong with Stephen,' TIM said. 'He has no fever, no infection markers and his vital signs are within normal parameters.'

'I don't call falling unconscious being within normal parameters!' Elizabeth said sharply. 'Shouldn't we get him to the hospital, John?'

John shook his head. 'You know as well as I do that Sap medicine is primitive compared to TIM's diagnostic capabilities. I didn't just program him with the sum knowledge of human medicine, I set

40

up his memory banks to be updated daily. Right now, there's nothing a hospital could do for Stephen. TIM's his best hope.'

Stephen's skin was a darker green now. He lay perfectly still, eyes closed, breathing deeply but steadily.

Elizabeth stroked his brow. 'He's been out of sorts for day. We had a stupid row the other night, when you were on your date.'

'A row? That's not like you two. What about?'

'Well, that's just it. It wasn't about anything in particular.'

'He was a bit off with me earlier too,' John admitted.

'Stephen's been acting strangely for days. I thought it was just teenage hormones. But ever since he started using the stone… I say, John, you don't think there could be a connection?'

John snorted. 'Are you suggesting that a transcendental meditation aid created by some of the world's leading neurologists, including I might add, someone I know personally, and endorsed by the World Society of Psychology, could have sent Stephen into a coma? I hardly think that's likely, Elizabeth.'

'Why not, John? We know very little about how these stones work. What I *do* know, having watched the kids use them at school, is that they're highly addictive and Stephen's been using his pretty much non-stop since he bought it. TIM, what do you think?'

'Elizabeth, you may have a point. As we've been talking, I've been monitoring the official news channels for the last hour, and there are reports from across the world of similar, unexplained illnesses. People are collapsing and falling into deep comas without any apparent cause. The hospitals are dangerously full, and Italy and France have just declared national emergencies. Other countries are likely to follow. There has been some panic on the streets.'

TIM's projection screen flickered into life and began to display footage of a busy shopping street. As John and Elizabeth watched, a man in a bowler hat fell to the ground and a crowd gathered around him. The image changed to the front of a hospital with a queue of ambulances waiting to unload patients at the Accident and Emergency entrance. Then the scene shifted to a riot, somewhere in southern Europe.

'What do you suggest, TIM?' John asked. 'If there is a connection between the Theta Mindstones and Stephen's condition, how do we get to the bottom of it?'

'I suggest we do a full medical scan of Stephen's brain.'

Elizabeth frowned. 'An X-Ray?'

'I believe TIM's proposing something rather more sophisticated than that, Elizabeth. Have you heard of Computed Tomography?'

'I'm afraid I haven't.'

'Well, that's not surprising,' John conceded. 'It's a fairly new invention. It's a type of scanner – where doctors take a series of X-Rays of someone's brain from different angles, and then put them together to create a three-dimensional image. TIM and I have taken that idea and created a portable version. Let me show you.'

He led Elizabeth into the Lab's research room and picked up a device the size and shape of a motorcycle helmet.

'That helmet can scan someone's head? You'll make a fortune,' Elizabeth said.

John smiled. 'Sadly, it only works if you can plug it into a biotronic computer. And I don't think we're ready to give the Saps access to the technology that makes TIM possible quite yet.'

They returned to the sleeping bay and John carefully slid the helmet over Stephen's unconscious head, before attaching a cable from the helmet into one of TIM's input sockets on the wall. The helmet buzzed for a few minutes and then bleeped. John ripped the print-out from TIM's printer and studied it on the central table.

He had tested the mobile CT helmet on himself half a dozen times during its development and was familiar with brain scans. TIM had printed a grid of images, each showing a cross section of Stephen's brain. The first couple were normal, but the third showed a circular white object in the left frontal cortex.

'It's an anomaly, possibly some kind of growth,' he told Elizabeth. 'TIM, can you create a three-dimensional image of the object and put it on the display?'

The screen flickered again, and then a new image came into focus. Elizabeth gasped. 'It's horrible.'

It appeared to be a living creature, almost identical to a nautilus, one of the most ancient aquatic organisms. Its spiral shell was smooth, and sticking out of the open end, protected by a hood, was an array of tentacles and a large eye. John was mesmerised by it, and appalled. Nothing like that should exist in a human brain.

'It seems to be some kind of cephalopod,' TIM said, 'around two centimetres in length.'

'How on Earth did it get inside Stephen?' Elizabeth asked. She didn't seem able to take her eyes off the image, either.

John made a deliberate effort to push aside his anxiety about Stephen. He needed to be a cool, rational scientist now if he was to save his friend. 'I can only speculate,' he said. 'But perhaps he was infected with the creature while using the stone.'

'That's impossible!' Elizabeth said.

'No, Elizabeth, it's not impossible,' TIM replied. 'There are creatures – alien creatures – that attach to their hosts through telepathic infiltration. They have the ability to use the amino acids and proteins that already exist in the host and manipulate them to create a living creature. It's rare, but it's not unknown.'

'What will happen to Stephen?' Elizabeth asked quietly, as if she was afraid of the answer.

'The parasite appears to be growing rapidly,' TIM said. He alone seemed entirely unemotional. John sometimes envied him his ability to remain calm in all circumstances. But of course, John had built him that way. 'Its tentacles are attaching themselves to vital parts of his brain. I estimate that at its current rate, it will pose a threat to his life within two hours.'

'We've got to get it out now! We've got to get him to a hospital,' Elizabeth said.

TIM's lights flashed as he replied. 'No human surgeon has the skill to remove such a complex creature in the time available without causing severe damage to Stephen's brain. The tentacles are interlinked in ways that are beyond medical science to detach.'

'Then what? We can't just sit and let him die.' Elizabeth's hands were clenched in frustration. It was harder for her, John realised. As someone without any real scientific knowledge, she must feel completely helpless in this situation.

'Could we remove it?' he asked TIM. 'Not through surgery, but through telekinesis. Could we sever its links to Stephen's brain? Once that was done, we could remove it manually.'

'That would be extremely risky, John.'

'But can it be done? Without an operation, Stephen will die.'

TIM paused, then said, 'I believe it might be possible. But the chances of failure are high.'

'Stephen's chances if we don't do it are even worse,' John said grimly. 'We have to try.'

5: Saviour Machine

Elizabeth could only watch, helplessly as John and TIM went to work.

TIM changed the image on his screen. Now it wasn't just showing the nautilus creature, but the whole of Stephen's brain around it. It made it far more horrible, seeing it that way. The nautilus looked like precisely what it was: a parasite, hooked into its victim.

There were fine threads running from the shell towards the tissues around it. One of them flashed red.

'Sever this link first, John,' TIM said. 'But you must be very careful not to damage the superior parietal lobule.'

Elizabeth felt John focus his powers, directing them with scalpel-like precision.

There was a brief, frightening pause, and then

TIM said, 'Well done, John. That link has been successfully broken.'

Another strand flashed red, and when John had severed that too, another. By the time he was working on the fourth, there were beads of sweat on his brow and his mouth was set in a tense, thin line.

'Maybe I can do some of it,' Elizabeth suggested.

'You don't know nearly enough about brain anatomy,' John said. 'You'd be as likely to hurt him as help him.' He'd spoken a little impatiently and Elizabeth did her best not to be wounded by it. She knew he was terribly worried about Stephen, and even more worried that his own actions might harm him.

She watched in silence as he detached strand after strand of the tendrils linking Stephen's brain to the creature that was killing it. When there were only two left, TIM suddenly snapped, 'John, you must stop immediately.'

For a second, it didn't seem as if John had heard him. Then he blinked and rubbed the sweat from his brow. 'I'm afraid I lost concentration for a moment.'

'And nearly destroyed Stephen's postcentral gyrus while you did,' TIM said, reprovingly.

'Maybe you should take a break,' Elizabeth suggested, but John shook his head.

'Stephen doesn't have time for me to sit around,' he said.

His face took on a look of intense concentration, and this time the final two strands were severed without difficulty.

'The procedure is complete,' TIM said. 'Excellent work, John. I believe you've saved Stephen's life.'

Elizabeth studied the brain scan, still floating on TIM's display. 'But the nautilus is still in there, isn't it? Don't you need to operate to remove it?'

'Oh, that's the easy part,' John said. 'Now that it's safely detached from his brain tissues.'

It might have been the easy part, but Elizabeth didn't particularly want to watch John cutting open Stephen's head. Now that she knew Stephen was safe, she withdrew to one of the secluded back rooms of the Lab to try to distract herself with a pile of marking. But it was impossible for her to concentrate, and after fifteen minutes she returned to the living area. When she did, she found Stephen resting peacefully on his bunk and John relaxing with a cup of tea.

'All done?' she asked.

John nodded.

'And Stephen's okay?'

John's expression grew more sombre. 'I'm afraid we won't know for sure until he wakes up. I thought

49

he would have regained consciousness by now. The anaesthetic has certainly worn off. If only we knew a little more about how those stones really work...'

'You could scan one, couldn't you, TIM?' Elizabeth asked. 'Look inside it the way you looked inside Stephen's head?'

'The matter of which the stone is constructed may be impervious to X-rays,' TIM said.

Elizabeth was rather deflated – she'd felt briefly as if she was a contributor rather than a spectator to John and TIM being awfully clever. But then John said, 'There's no harm in trying, TIM. Even if you *can't* scan it, that will tell us something.'

He picked up the stone from the sofa and placed it carefully on the circular tabletop in the middle of the living area.

'Very well, please stand back from the stone as I scan it,' TIM said, his lights flashing. There was a hum, and the lights brightened – until all at once, there was a high-pitched whine which forced Elizabeth and Stephen to cover their ears and TIM's lights went out. At exactly the same time, every other light in the Lab went out too. The room was plunged into absolute darkness. Elizabeth couldn't even see her own hand, let alone John, or TIM.

The whine stopped and the Lab was silent. 'What's going—' she said, and before she could finish the sentence, the lights came back on again.

But they weren't the same as before. The glow coming out of them wasn't a comforting white but an awful, sickly green. It looked like the colour of the sea, when you were very far beneath it.

'TIM?' John said, and then again, more loudly, 'TIM, answer me!'

TIM's lights flashed, and they too were a different colour, the yellows and greens of mould and other, viler things. 'Who is TIM?' he asked. 'There is no TIM here.'

'I'll have to run a diagnostic,' John said gravely. His face looked wrong in the ugly green light. It looked as if it had started to decay. He reached for the panel of controls at TIM's base – and an arc of electricity connected with his hand before it could touch anything.

He yelled in pain and snatched his hand away. Then he reached out tentatively with just one finger, but the same thing happened again.

'John, stop,' Elizabeth said. 'You'll hurt yourself.'

'What on Earth is going on?' John asked, his normally calm facade beginning to crack. He tapped at some controls near TIM's base and then frowned at the wavy lines that appeared on the screen. 'I don't understand. TIM's programme is based on my brain – and his brainwave pattern should mirror mine. But it's changed beyond recognition. It's as if there are two minds occupying the same physical space. Which is impossible. And another thing. According to my manual diagnostic, TIM's reacting very much like a computer that's been presented with a paradox.'

'What do you mean?'

'If a normal computer is given two conflicting instructions, or two pieces of information that can't exist at the same time, its programming can get trapped in an endless loop. It freezes. And that seems to be what's happened with TIM. But he isn't an ordinary computer. He's biotronic and his mind should be able to cope with a paradox. That's what makes him so flexible and creative. This makes no sense.'

As he spoke, the whine started again. It was coming from TIM, and this time Elizabeth recognised it. It was the same sound that the Theta Mindstone had made when Stephen had been bothered by the silverfish the other day, but amplified to the point of discomfort.

'What's wrong with him?' Elizabeth shouted to

John, over the horrible noise. 'He almost sounds as if he's in pain.'

'That shouldn't be possible! He shouldn't be able to feel pain.'

'Should we turn him off? At least until we can figure out what's wrong.'

'Good idea,' John said. TIM did not have a on-off button like conventional computers, but there was a switch that controlled the power to his speech and transmission circuits. John pulled open the metal hatch that revealed the green light indicating TIM was active. He reached for the master switch—

—and in the moment that he touched it, everything went black. Elizabeth felt the familiar, wrenching sensation of jaunting. But she hadn't done it. Someone had done it to her. And as light began to glow around her, she saw that she was completely alone. She and John had been separated, and flung somewhere away from the Lab. But where?

6: Unwashed and Somewhat Slightly Dazed

Something was different. Stephen lay on the bed, his eyes closed, desperately trying to focus his thoughts, which felt like they were swimming in treacle. There was a dull ache at the back of his skull, and he felt a strong urge to sink back to oblivion.

'*TIM,*' he forced himself to call out with this mind. '*TIM, are you there?*'

There was no reply. He slowly eased open his eyelids to confirm that he was where he should be. It was the Lab all right, but something was different. In his disorientated state he couldn't work out what.

He lay on the bed, concentrating on his breathing. The head pain was there, but it was getting easier. And it was a different sort of ache from the headache he'd been experiencing for the last week. This was sharper, less sickly. He didn't think the problem he was sensing was in him.

He sat up and looked around the Lab. The furniture was all there. TIM's tubes and globes were hanging over him from the ceiling. The white brick walls of the old Underground Tunnel were the same. But the light was now a sickly green. And, more alarming, TIM was silent.

Normally, even when TIM wasn't speaking, Stephen could sense his comforting presence in the room, hear the gentle ticking and swirling. But now there was nothing. It was as if TIM had been switched off.

'Elizabeth, John? Are you there?' He sent the message out without speaking. There was no reply. They had all vanished. Were they asleep? Or on another planet? It was impossible to know. He pulled off the sheet and slowly, painfully sat up. The Lab was empty, and he was completely alone.

John's eyes blinked open sleepily. The blanket was scratchy against his chest, but the bed was comfortable, and he was tempted to go back to sleep.

Wait. Why was he in bed? He'd been in the Lab a moment ago, hadn't he? And then… he struggled to recall. Yes, he'd been jaunted away involuntarily, separated from Elizabeth and sent here, wherever here was.

He pushed the blanket away and sat up. The lighting was dim, but not so dim that he couldn't make out his surroundings. He seemed to be in a wooden cabin of some sort, maybe a beach hut or a holiday home. Except, running across the ceiling there was a red wire as thick as his arm. It looked both familiar and out of place.

The curtains were closed, so he couldn't see the view outside the window. He tossed aside the blanket and rose to go and open them, then stopped, astonished, when he noticed what he was wearing.

Astronaut pyjamas? That was absurd. He hadn't owned anything like them since he was a little boy. And he definitely hadn't changed out of his clothes before being jaunted here. He looked behind him and saw that the bed he'd been sleeping in was actually a bunk bed. He must have barely fitted on it – it looked as if it was designed for a toddler.

Well, he could solve the mystery of his clothes later. The important thing was to establish where exactly he was, who'd sent him there and why.

He pulled back the bright blue curtain over the window, but it was night outside, too cloudy for any moonlight to penetrate. He could have been anywhere.

If he went out of the door, he might well walk straight into his captors. And that was if they'd been foolish enough to leave it unlocked. But it was harder to capture a Tomorrow Person than that: mere walls couldn't hold him. He focused his mind, intending to jaunt the short hop from inside to outside the cabin, where the dark night would hide him from any watching eyes. He reached for that sense inside himself that Saps didn't have, the muscle that wasn't a muscle...

He felt nothing. He hadn't moved anywhere. Whoever had jaunted him here had made sure he couldn't jaunt out again.

There was nothing for it, he'd have to try the door. He walked quietly over to it. There were voices outside. Raised voices, arguing by the sound of it. That was useful. If he listened, he might pick up a clue about his captors. And the voices *did* sound familiar. Was this some enemy he'd faced before?

Then, with a lurching shock, he realised why he recognised them. He was listening to his own parents' voices. He felt a strong and inexplicable urge to back away. He knew he didn't want to hear what they were saying, what they were arguing about. He'd do anything not to hear it...

He'd backed away from the door three paces before he regained control of himself. This was ridiculous. This wasn't his home. If his parents were outside, he needed to know why. He had to discover if they'd been captured too. He reached for the door handle...

Elizabeth opened her eyes to a landscape she'd never seen before. She seemed to be at the bottom of a valley, but the ground was a hard, smooth white, like nothing that existed on Earth. Had she been jaunted to an alien planet? If she had, it wasn't one she'd ever visited previously. Her hair was being blown by a cool breeze. It wasn't like any wind she'd experienced before. This was unchanging and unrelenting.

She knelt to examine the peculiar ground more closely. It was cracked, but not like normal soil. There was some sort of black goo in the cracks. No wonder she could see no trees growing, no plants at all. It was nothing but this strange white substance in every direction she looked. The planet appeared to be completely barren.

Still, there might be landmarks that would help her to identify it. It was impossible to say from down here in the valley. She needed to get to the top of the hill, where she should be able to see for miles.

The climb was very hard. Her platform shoes couldn't get a very good grip on the smooth white ground. Twice she fell and slipped, losing yards of ground that she'd so arduously gained. But finally, she managed to reach the peak of the hill.

There was nothing to see. Nothing but more white valleys and white hills, stretching into infinity in every direction. Except they weren't really hills, they were more like very, very long ridges, so long she couldn't see the end of them. She couldn't even see a horizon. It was as if the surface of the planet curved up instead of down, but that was completely impossible.

But there was something, she realised, other than the relentless white. In the distance there was a black dot, growing rapidly closer. Soon it was close enough for her to see some of its features. It had translucent wings and big, multi-faceted eyes. It was hideous and it was flying straight towards her.

She backed away from the brow of the ridge, where she'd be a clear target for the creature, whatever it was. But it simply rose higher in the air to keep her in view. And now it was even closer she could see its slender, multi-jointed legs and the coarse hairs on them.

It looked exactly like a house fly, but hundreds of times bigger than it should be. And it was still heading towards her. Its monstrous proboscis extended towards her, a viscous liquid dripping from its tip.

She tried to jaunt away, to one of the more distant ridges, far from the monstrous fly. She concentrated, the way she always did, but nothing happened. She didn't move an inch. Something was stopping her jaunting. Her only option was to escape the old-fashioned way.

She turned away, ready to flee – and saw that her way back was blocked too. Behind and to her left, two vast silver shapes were approaching, moving over the ground rather than through the air, but at an incredible speed. And they were every bit as hideous as the huge fly. Their bodies were long and segmented, and they had two long antennae protruding from their heads, waving through the air as if they were searching for something.

They looked just like giant silverfish. A giant fly? Giant silverfish? What was going on?

'Species identified, *Drosophila melanogaster*,' a huge voice boomed out. It wasn't coming from the silverfish. It seemed to be coming from the sky itself. 'Species marked for eradication. Engage termination protocols.'

The two silverfish had reached the giant fly. As Elizabeth watched, fascinated and appalled, nozzles emerged from between their jaws and a green liquid jetted out, covering the fly in moments. Everywhere it touched the fly's flesh, the flesh dissolved, until very soon there was nothing left of it but a pile of revolting gunk.

Elizabeth stood as still as she could. She tried to breathe shallowly, so that even her breaths wouldn't make any noise, and for a moment it seemed to be working. The silverfish were moving away. They were ignoring her.

The voice boomed out again. 'Species identified. *Homo superior*. Species marked for extermination. Engage eradication protocols.'

The two silverfish swung round, until their antennae were facing Elizabeth. She took one look at them, then turned and ran.

7: When I Live My Dream

John opened the door – and walked through it into a huge hall. He was on the stage and in front of him were rows and rows of wooden seats, filled with children in school uniform. *His* school uniform, or the one he'd worn for grammar school, anyway. And this was his school hall, smelling slightly of mothballs, the way it always had. This should have been good news: his school wasn't very far from the Lab. But he was beginning to believe that in the place he'd been brought, wherever it really was, appearances could be deceptive.

There was a podium on the stage. His headmaster was standing behind it, wearing his gown and an academic cap over his shiny bald head. The pupils used to call him Mr Magoo, but never to his face.

'And I'd like you all to give a big round of applause,' the headmaster said, 'for John, at eleven years old, the youngest ever student to gain his O-Level in Physics.'

There was a sound from the audience, but it wasn't clapping. It was a gale of loud, mocking laughter. John cringed at it, as if he was still the boy who'd been teased by his schoolmates for being too clever for his own good. He looked across the hall, at the ranks and ranks of seated pupils. The laughter was definitely coming from that direction, and yet their mouths weren't moving. Their faces were completely expressionless.

John tried to locate the source of the laughter. He looked around for hidden speakers, up towards the ceiling – and had to squint his eyes shut against the very bright light that was coming from above. It was as bright as a floodlight, but it was flashing, in a way that no flashlight would, and as it flashed the colour changed: white to green to blue to red. There was something very familiar about it. If only John's head were clearer, he might be able to...

'To accept the certificate on his behalf, please let me introduce John's parents.'

John's stomach lurched with fear. He hadn't noticed his parents, standing beside the headmaster. Had they even been there, before he said their names?

John's dad came up to the podium, wearing his police sergeant's uniform, but he didn't face the audience. He turned to John's mother instead and said, 'Don't be daft. It's all in your mind, Margaret!'

'It's not!' his mother said. She sounded almost hysterical. 'I'm telling you, he can hear—'

No. No. It was the same conversation, the same argument they'd been having in the wooden chalet. John refused to hear it. He had to get away from it. He ran to the back of the stage, ripped the curtain aside – and found himself somewhere else entirely.

He'd been standing before. Now he was sitting, on a pedalo in a lake. His legs were tired, as if he'd been pedalling for a long time, even though he'd only just arrived. And he knew that he had to keep going, he had to speed up. He knew, without knowing how he knew, that he was being chased, and that if he was caught, something very bad would happen.

In contrast to the furious motion of his legs, the lake was tranquil. It was ringed with weeping willows and, a short distance away, a white swan was leading her cygnets through the water. This was another place he recognised, although he didn't know it as well as his old school. It was the boating lake near his aunt and uncle's house in Kent. He used to be sent there during the school holidays, 'for a change of scene' his mother used to say.

There was the splash of an oar behind him. Whoever was chasing him was catching up. He risked stopping pedalling for a moment to glance over his shoulder. It was a rowing boat, only twenty yards or so behind him. There were two figures inside it, pulling at the oars. Their heads were bent, their faces shadowed. Then, as if sensing John's eyes on them, they both looked up.

It was his parents again. He'd known it would be. He tried to pedal faster, to get away, but it was getting harder, as if the water itself was resisting him. Except… it wasn't water, not anymore. It was thick and green and iridescent, like oil.

Of course! Finally, it all snapped into place. The red wire, the lights, the oil. Now John knew exactly where he must be, and exactly what he needed to do to escape.

The giant silverfish had almost caught up with Elizabeth. She could hear the click-clacking of their metallic feet on the hard white ground, and a horrible, high-pitched chittering coming out of their mouths.

She knew what they'd do if they caught her. She'd seen it happen to the fly. They'd spit acid that would dissolve her down to her constituent molecules.

They were almost close enough to do it now. She imagined their mouths opening, the liquid bubbling...

But there! To her left there was a tunnel, burrowing into the white ground. It was far too narrow for the silverfish to fit through. Elizabeth flung herself towards it, not even worrying about what could be inside. It was bound to be better than the silverfish.

Just as she'd entered the tunnel, she heard the hiss of liquid coming from the silverfish's mouth. A few drops splashed inside the tunnel, steaming where they landed and causing white ground to bubble and melt.

Elizabeth shuddered and moved hurriedly away from them. It was too dark to see very much, but the ground here felt different. Was that grass, growing beneath her feet? She could definitely feel something brushing against her legs as she walked.

It was getting darker as she moved further in, though. Pretty soon she wouldn't be able to see her own hand in front of her face. She should probably stop, wait until the silverfish lost interest, and then go back outside again. She took one final step forward – and then cried out in shock as the ground fell away beneath her.

She reached out desperately for the grass – or whatever it was – as she fell. It didn't feel like grass at all. It seemed to be moving all on its own. Disgusted, she let go of the tenuous hold she had on it.

It seemed to go on and on, falling into darkness. The strange organic growths brushed against her as she plummeted. They must have slowed her down enough, because when she finally reached the bottom, she fell onto her backside with a painful bump, but the impact was no worse than that. Nothing was broken.

She looked around and groaned. She seemed to have got precisely nowhere. She was in another endless white landscape of smooth ridges and empty valleys. And there, in the far distance, she could see shapes moving that she was very much afraid were more silverfish.

It was peculiar to feel trapped in such a wide-open space, but she did. There was no sun to see, no clouds – just a misty whiteness overhead and the ridges rolling on and on, curving improbably up into the distance, while that constant wind blew in her face.

And all at once she knew why she felt confined. It was because she *was* inside. She couldn't believe it had taken her this long to recognise where she was. She'd seen it every day for the last month, hanging above her head in the Lab. But, of course, it did look rather different from the outside.

She didn't know how it had happened or why, but she was now sure that she was *inside* TIM, or rather inside his biofluid connectors, the white translucent tubes that she had seen so often on the ceiling of the Lab. John had told her once that the fluid was carried in the walls of the tubes, and that the centres of the tubes were hollow to allow cooling air to pass through TIM's systems. She must have been shrunk down to a fraction of her normal size. She hadn't even known that was possible, but in a universe in which people could jump through space in the blink of an eye and move objects with their minds, it didn't seem that outlandish.

The mechanical silverfish must be part of TIM's automatic defence system. Now she thought about it, she remembered him mentioning it a few days ago. They were used to clean dirt and other debris from his circuits.

If John were here, he'd know what to do. She let herself feel a moment's panic, then made herself suppress it. John wasn't here, and she was, and she might not know everything he did about science, but she still had a mind. She needed to use it.

Yes, she remembered now! Just before they'd been separated, John had spoken about paradoxes, the way they could be used to trap a simple computer in an endless loop. And these silverfish seemed pretty simple. They were only subsystems, nothing like as intelligent as TIM himself. At least she hoped so!

She felt suddenly much calmer. She knew what to do. If she kept her head, and acted fast, she could still get out of this.

8: All The Madmen

Stephen stood in the centre of the darkened Lab, beneath the tubes and hemispheres of a silent TIM, and wondered what to do. He rubbed the back of his head and winced with a sharp pain. There was a cut or scratch that hadn't been there before. What on Earth had happened to him? The last thing he remembered was talking to John and Elizabeth in the Lab. He looked at his watch. That was over three hours ago.

'Well, you're not going to achieve anything moping around here on your own,' he told himself. If the others had abandoned him, there must have been an emergency. He looked around for a note but could see nothing other than some computer printouts on the glass table.

He studied them intensely. It took him a few seconds to recognise that he was looking at scans of a human brain. But something wasn't quite right in one of the scans. In the left hemisphere was a familiar white swirl. He held it closer. The swirl resembled a seashell, but there were tentacles poking out from the open edge. The thought of something like that inside a human brain made him feel nauseous. The other scan showed a normal brain without the creature.

Wait, was that writing around the edge of the image? He peered more closely, and with a thudding shock, saw his own name. This wasn't just any brain scan – this was an image of *his* brain.

'TIM, TIM, can you hear me?' he called out. 'Can you tell me what's been happening? TIM?'

There was no reply.

Was that thing, that seashell thing, still inside his head? He went to the bathroom and lifted up the shaving mirror so he could examine the top of his head. There, around the same place where his head hurt, was a tiny area of shaved hair, and a red weal – as if someone had made a cut and then somehow healed it up again without stitches.

But had the cut been used to insert the creature, or remove it? He looked again at the images. TIM had timestamped each of them – and the one without the creature was an hour later. So the others had scanned his brain, found the creature, and somehow taken it out. But where were they now?

None of this made any sense. But he knew where he had seen the seashell shape. It was the same as the spiral logo on the packaging of the Theta Mindstone. It couldn't be a coincidence. And with a horrible prickling sensation at the back of his neck, Stephen began to piece together what must have happened.

The stones were more than just a relaxation aid – somehow, they had infected him with that... He couldn't bring himself to look at the scan again. And Elliot Jackson? Stephen felt sick at the thought of him, and foolish too. He'd fallen for his charm, and his cheek. The man was a hypocrite; John had been right, and Stephen had been too blinded by celebrity. He didn't know what Jackson was up to, but it wasn't good. And if there were any answers to be had, they wouldn't be found here, but at the Elliot Jackson Institute.

Getting there presented a problem, though. Without TIM to guide his jaunts, Stephen needed alternative transport to get to Hertfordshire. Luckily, there was one person who might be able to help.

Not many Saps knew who the Tomorrow People were, but there were a few trusted friends who were in on the secret. Stephen just hoped he'd be able to catch the one he wanted at home. He made the call from the phone box close to the secret entrance to the Lab.

Chris answered on the second ring. 'Go on, what do you need now?'

'Well, I wouldn't ask if it wasn't urgent, Chris. Can you borrow your brother Ginge's motorbike? I need a lift to Hertfordshire.'

'Can't you use your special powers and teleport there?'

'I wish I could. But TIM's shut down and John and Elizabeth have vanished. I'm on my own.'

Chris sighed good-humouredly. 'All right, it's not like I've got a life of my own or anything. I'll be there in fifteen minutes.'

London's streets were eerily quiet. As they rode through the suburbs, Stephen could see figures lying in gardens or on the pavements, apparently asleep or unconscious. Again and again, he spotted half a leg sticking out from a doorway, or saw a driver slumped in their car. He wanted to stop and help but knew he couldn't.

'What's happening?' Chris shouted behind him as they sped through north London.

'It's the Theta Mindstones. They're knocking people out,' Stephen shouted back.

'Never used one myself. My problem isn't relaxing, it's getting out of bed.'

An hour and a half later, Stephen – windswept, tousled and still shaking from the ride – was standing outside the perimeter wall of the Elliot Jackson Institute.

'Now what?' Chris asked excitedly.

'Well, now I jaunt in. A TP can do a small jaunt of a few hundred yards without TIM's help. It's the ones over distance that are too difficult.'

Chris looked disappointed. 'But what about me?'

'Sorry, Chris, but there's no way to get you in safely. The guards are armed and they're not particularly friendly to strangers. Best thing is for you to stay here. I might need a quick getaway.'

'First, I'm your taxi driver, now you want me to be your getaway driver? Glad I'm useful for something.' But Stephen could see that he was only joking. 'So where are you going to jaunt to?'

Stephen had been thinking about this on the journey up from London. Without TIM's help, there was a danger of jaunting into a solid object, so he needed to reach out with his mind to locate an open space.

'Well, it's past six so the factory floor should be quiet and it's the biggest open space in the building,' he told Chris.

'Sounds risky to me,' Chris replied. 'You'll probably jaunt next to a tea lady and give her the scare of her life. But your choice.'

'It is. And stay here. Don't do anything stupid.'

Stephen materialised in the corner of the factory floor. By sheer luck he'd jaunted to a secluded corner of the packing area, hidden from view by stacks of cardboard boxes waiting to be loaded onto lorries in the morning. The factory floor was dark and quiet – the only sound was that of flowing water that seemed to come from the floor below.

He crept out from behind the boxes. Yes, the floor was deserted and the conveyor belt that spiralled around the factory was still. He ducked underneath the belt and made his way to the centre of the room, where the conveyor emerged from a hole in the floor. The sound of rushing water was louder here, and flickers of light were coming from the basement.

He peered over the edge of the floor into the room below and his eyes widened in surprise. It was the same size as the factory floor but was covered in a glistening layer of what looked like yellow jelly. The smell was overpowering and reminded Stephen of rotten fish and decaying seaweed. He forced himself not to vomit, and gingerly began to clamber down the conveyor belt into the murk below.

It wasn't as hard as he'd feared. There were solid wooden ridges which acted like steps taking him down. He tried to move as silently as he could but was conscious of the clattering of the belt as he shifted his weight. The floor was at least sixty feet below him and he paused halfway to get his bearings. The noise of rushing water grew louder with every step he took.

The light down there was patchy, and it took his eyes a few moments to acclimatise. But he could see that something shadowy at the far end of the basement was pulsating, sending ripples of light out through the jelly-like substance that spread across the floor. In places the jelly was several thick feet. He peered again, and as his eyes adjusted to the darkness, the shape took form.

It was a gigantic nautilus, at least forty feet tall, suspended in a vast glass tank of water and steel. The tank appeared to be completely sealed and from what Stephen could see, its walls were inches thick. Inside, the shell was striped red and white, and partly translucent, revealing a throbbing mass of limbs and writhing tissue inside it. Stephen felt sick at the memory that something just like that had been inside his own brain.

The head sticking out of the shell was protected by the upper half of a triangular beak. From below the beak, a vast flat eye peered out through a ring of twisting tentacles that seemed to be exploring the water in front of the creature.

Stephen had never seen anything so terrifying and yet so mesmerising. He watched, transfixed, as a tube descended from the creature's head and slithered lazily to the floor of the tank.

The tube bulged, and slowly a white blob was squeezed out of it. It looked like an eye the size of a large potato. A mechanical claw emerged from the jelly in the floor of the tank and pulled the blob through a hatch and into a smaller metal cylinder attached to the side. The hatch doors closed and there was a hissing, bubbling sound. Two people, dressed in protective plastic suits and masks, approached the cylinder, opened it up and removed the object, laying it carefully in a trough alongside dozens of others. They were eggs, Stephen realised. The creature, whatever it was, was giving birth. And the smaller cylinder seemed to be some kind of decompression tank. The pressure inside the large tank must be fantastic, he thought.

He looked around the room and for the first time saw hundreds upon hundreds of troughs, all filled with the white blobs. *They're stones,* thought Stephen with horror. *The stones are this creature's eggs.* And once again he felt a wash of shame through his body as he recalled how much he'd been taken in by Jackson.

He shifted his weight to get a better look, and then felt himself slip. Helplessly, he clattered down the conveyor belt, unable to get a grip on the wooden slats, feeling them bang into his back and bottom one by one. After a few seconds he came to a stop, but his cover had been blown.

The nautilus creature emitted a penetrating shriek and from nowhere, a dozen guards appeared, pointing and raising their weapons. Time to go, Stephen thought, and jaunted to the factory floor as the sound of gunfire echoed from below. If he'd still been down there, he would have been dead.

He felt a moment of relief – but it didn't last long. Standing a few feet away were four figures. Two were armed guards. One was Elliot Jackson dressed in his tie-dye T-shirt. And the fourth was his friend Chris.

Jackson spoke. Gone was the chummy voice from the other day, replaced with something colder and more dangerous. The Mockney accent had vanished too. 'Very impressive. Some kind of teleportation, I guess? Well, try that again, Mr Jameson, and I'm afraid we'll have to shoot your pal here.'

9: Can't Help Thinking About Me

The giant silverfish had almost reached Elizabeth. She could hear the clattering of their metal feet on the white ground and knew that they must be less than a hundred feet away, but she didn't look up. All her concentration was focused on her painting.

She was using the black goo that oozed from cracks in the white floor. When she'd realised she needed something as paint, she'd thought of it immediately. She didn't have a paintbrush, so she was using her fingers. The goo was horribly sticky, but it was working. She'd almost finished. The eye was done, and most of the head. All she had left to add was the most important bit: the two long, thin shapes that might have been ears, or might have been two halves of a beak.

The silverfish were so close now, she could smell them: a sharp, stinging scent that probably came from their acid weapons. In seconds they'd be spraying it on her, but she'd done it. One final artistic swirl of her finger and the painting was done.

She leapt back out of the way, making sure to give the silverfish a clear view of what she'd created. They looked even more horrible close up, their segmented bodies slithering behind them as they moved and their antennae twitching.

As they barrelled towards her, she felt a sick flash of doubt. Did she really think a stupid art project could stop TIM's automated defences? But it was too late now. She closed her eyes and waited for the worst to happen.

After several moments when nothing had, she opened them again.

It had worked! The giant silverfish were immobile, their insectile eyes wide and staring at her painting. It was an optical illusion: a black-and white picture of something that could look like a duck, or a rabbit, depending on how your brain decided to see it. With some effort, she could make her own flick between the two options, first seeing a blunt face with two ears streaming behind, then a narrow head ending in a beak: rabbit, duck, rabbit, duck.

That must be what was happening inside the silverfish's mechanical minds, too. But because she was human, she could understand what she was seeing, that it was both things at once. They were trapped forever between the two options.

She wasn't John. She couldn't reprogramme the silverfish. So she'd created a visual paradox instead. She might not have the same skills and knowledge as her friend, she reminded herself, but she had her own, and they were every bit as useful.

The silverfish were out of commission. That was one problem solved. Now all she needed to do was find a way out.

John now knew where he was with certainty. He was trapped in TIM's telepathic circuits. He didn't know how on Earth he could have been shrunk down and brought there but, as Sherlock Holmes said, 'When you have excluded the impossible, whatever remains, however improbable, must be the truth.'

Something must have happened to TIM, corrupted him. Because, improbable as it seemed, it must be TIM himself who was working against John. He'd taken memories from inside John's own head to build this illusory, ever-shifting prison. John had made TIM using his own mind as a model. It hadn't occurred to John at the time that this would give TIM easy access to parts of his memory that he'd never intended to share, or revisit.

There must be a reason that TIM was throwing these particular visions at John. He was using them to drive John away. Every time John approached somewhere TIM didn't want him to be, he was presented with a vision of his parents, a memory of that horrible argument that he'd tried so very hard to forget.

But he couldn't hide from it any longer. Wherever TIM didn't want him to be was clearly exactly where he needed to be. He had to face his fears.

He felt a surge of anger, at TIM and at himself for being so easily manipulated. But these were *his* memories, and he could control them. He closed his eyes, concentrated hard on where he wanted to be, and when he opened them, he was in the wooden chalet again.

He knew exactly where it was now. It was a Butlins camp in Bognor Regis. His parents had brought him there on holiday when he was four. It had been wet and windy and they'd had to spend most of their time indoors. His mum and dad had been irritable with him and snappy with each other.

And on the last day, he'd woken up to hear them arguing outside his room.

He could hear them now. Their voices were muffled by the door. When he'd been four, he'd pressed his ear against it to hear what they were saying. But this wasn't really Butlins and John knew that he needed to do more. He needed to step through the door to reach the part of TIM's circuits that TIM was blocking him from.

Even so, he hesitated with his hand on the doorknob. He hadn't thought about this memory in a long time. He hadn't let himself. Some things were too painful. He drew in a deep breath to steady himself and opened the door.

His parents looked so young. They were standing very close together, glaring at each other. They didn't look up when John emerged from his room. He knew this was because he wasn't really there. In reality, child John had never come out of the room. His parents never knew that he'd overheard them.

'I'm frightened of him, George,' his mother said.

His father made a scoffing sound. 'You're being ridiculous. He's four years old!'

'But he's not a normal four-year-old. Don't pretend you can't see it! I know you think so too.' His mother looked on the point of tears.

'He's cleverer than most, I'll give you that. We're raising a little genius. We should be proud, Margaret!'

John wished he could stop there, with the moment his father had defended him. But he knew he needed to let the whole memory play out. It was the only way to break through TIM's illusion.

'He's not just clever,' his mum said. She was crying properly now. Her face was red and splotchy. 'He's spooky. Sometimes it's as if I can feel him inside my own head, listening to my thoughts! The way he looks at me, George... like he thinks he's better than me. Cleverer than me. And he is! He isn't a little boy. I don't know what he is – something unnatural.'

'For god's sake, Margaret, don't be so daft. He's just a baby.'

John wanted to close his eyes. He wanted to cover his ears so he wouldn't need to hear the next part. But he knew he had to.

'I'm ashamed to admit it,' his mum said, 'but I don't know if I love him. I'm not sure I ever have.'

At those words, the world began to shimmer, as if John was seeing it through water, or tears. And when he blinked his eyes to clear them, his mum and dad disappeared. The chalet dissolved into nothing, and what was left behind was a plastic tube and a huge tangle of wiring. John was in TIM's electronic amygdala.

And there, standing the other side of it, was Elizabeth. She looked shaken, but unharmed. John was very relieved that she seemed to be alright. But if she was, TIM wasn't.

Wrapped around his amygdala, around all of those wires and circuits, was another nautilus. It throbbed with a sickly green light.

'Welcome John, welcome Elizabeth,' a voice said. It sounded a little like TIM, but far less friendly, and it seemed to be coming out of the nautilus itself. 'Welcome to the last moment of your existence.'

And then, far fainter, another voice. TIM's real voice. 'John. Elizabeth. Please. Help me.'

10: Hang On to Yourself

One moment Elizabeth had been running across the undulating white landscape of TIM's biofluid connectors, the next she had found herself in this space: in his electronic heart. She was delighted to find John here too.

She stared, horrified, at the nautilus. It was one of the most disgusting things she had ever seen. Encrusted in slime and emitting a sickly olive green light, its tentacles were weaving and pulsing around Tim's nerve centre. Elizabeth didn't like the thought of touching it, but she reached out for it anyway, intending to rip it away.

'No, Elizabeth!' John said sharply. 'If you tear if off, you could kill him. Remember what happened with Stephen. It's integrated with TIM on a psychic level. It must have formed its connection with TIM when he scanned it in the Lab. The only way to save him, is to sever the telepathic link between them, as well as the physical one.'

'John, Elizabeth,' TIM said, in a voice so feeble they could barely hear it. 'Use your emotions. Draw on the things that you've been made to face.'

'I'm afraid it's far too late to help him,' the other voice said, the darker one that was almost but not quite like TIM's. 'Our plans have almost reached fruition. You won't be able to stop us now.'

'We've cured Stephen,' John said. 'We can certainly cure everyone else. I think you'll find we're rather more resourceful than you anticipate.'

'Ah, but we're not working alone,' the creature said.

'No, that dreadful Elliot Jackson is working for you, isn't he?' Elizabeth said.

'Not for us. We are working together. My mother made contact with him many years ago, according to your human calendar, when his mind had been freed of the shackles of his flesh.'

'When he was high on hallucinogenic drugs, I should imagine,' John said disapprovingly.

The nautilus's light glowed a deeper green. 'Humans such as him are not equipped to communicate across the vast distances between species. The substances he took opened doors that are usually closed. They allowed his mind to reach a place where words aren't needed, and so we came to know each other completely.'

'But why on Earth would he agree to help you?' Elizabeth asked. 'What is he getting out of it?'

'Power,' John said. 'Wealth. All the things he claims not to care about.'

'You do him a disservice,' the nautilus said. There was a hint of annoyance in its voice, as if John had offended it. 'He is a visionary. He sees a world without war, or suffering.'

'He sees a world without free will, or individualism,' John countered.

The creature ignored him. 'With his help, my mother was able to make the leap to your world, from ours. The crossing was painful. It was nearly fatal. But it was worth every moment of pain. For with Elliot's help, we will bring new life to this world. *My siblings,* a hundred thousand of them, growing inside the fertile soil of your brains.'

'That's horrible!' Elizabeth said. 'People aren't your seed beds!'

'Aren't they? You humans have had your chance on this planet, and you've wasted it. Your brains have so much potential, and yet in the million years since you climbed out of the trees, you've barely scratched the surface of what they can achieve. Look at humanity now. Most of you are starving, poor, sick, terrified – and the rest of you allow it to happen while you fill your lives shopping, watching television, sleeping, fighting, drinking. It's pathetic. If you're not going to use the full potential of your brains, then it's time to hand them over to someone who will.'

'You, I suppose,' Elizabeth said.

'Why not? We will use the brains and bodies of humanity to enrich the universe. All I need to do is silence your minds long enough for my siblings' telepathic tendrils to take root. And you make it so very easy for us. All these millions of humans, desperate to quieten the voices inside their own heads. Learning to meditate, to make themselves into a void. We're only giving you what you want, after all: serenity.'

'Not serenity,' John said. 'Obliteration.'

The creature's tendrils writhed as it spoke. 'Two words for the same thing. We will scoop out the minds of humanity and fill the emptiness with my siblings, and there is nothing you can do to stop us.'

'Emptiness!' Elizabeth said, everything suddenly snapping into place. 'John, that's it. That thing needs people's minds to be empty before it can take hold. It can't deal with strong emotions.'

John nodded. 'I believe you're right, Elizabeth. It's a little like the way a computer floppy disc works. It has to be blank in order for you to write over it. If there's something already there, you have to erase it first. But you can't erase a feeling *while* it's being felt.'

'Idle speculation!' the nautilus said. But Elizabeth thought there was a note of panic in its voice.

'Remember what I showed you,' TIM gasped, as if speaking cost him a huge amount of effort.

'Of course!' John looked intently at Elizabeth. 'I don't know what you've been through since we were jaunted here, but whatever it was, it was designed to elicit a strong emotion. Whatever that emotion was, try to remember what that felt like – relive it if you can.'

It wasn't easy. The emotion Elizabeth had felt was terror. But that had been when she was being chased by two monsters out of her worst nightmares. Standing here, with John beside her, she wasn't afraid. So, she made herself think about what would happen if they failed. Millions of humans turned into mindless hosts for these creatures. She and John stuck here inside TIM forever. TIM himself deleted for good and replaced by this awful creature.

The fear came rushing back and she projected it outward, towards the nautilus that had TIM in its grip. She could see the concentration on John's face as he did the same. She wondered what feeling *he* was summoning up. It didn't matter. The important thing was to make that creature feel what they were feeling – to confront it with all the strong, messy human emotions that it was determined to erase.

The air was pierced with a high, desperate psychic scream that got louder and louder. The green light from the nautilus was growing ever brighter too as it struggled to resist the emotional onslaught.

Keep going, Elizabeth told herself, keep going. She focused harder, reliving the frustration and fear she had felt earlier in the biofluid connectors. And it was working. The scream grew louder, the light brighter, and then, there was a feeling like an explosion of light in Elizabeth's mind. She shut her eyes instinctively, even though she knew the light was an illusion.

As she did, she felt that peculiar wrenching sensation that always accompanied a jaunt. And when she opened her eyes again, it was to see the familiar surroundings of the Lab.

John was standing beside her. 'TIM!' he said urgently. 'Can you hear me? Are you, well, you?'

Elizabeth watched with enormous relief as the lights she'd come to know so well flashed their usual warm colours. There was a pause, and then a sound that was almost like TIM clearing his throat. 'I am quite well, thank you, John,' TIM said.

'We've done it,' she said. 'But I'm utterly drained.' And then she looked around the Lab. 'Stephen! Where's Stephen gone.'

'I'm not sure, Elizabeth. I'll need a moment to locate him.'

There was a pause and Elizabeth imagined TIM's powerful telepathic mind sweeping the streets above their head for the tell-tale signature of Stephen's brain, then across the city and then further afield.

'I've found him,' TIM said, and this time there was a note of urgency in his voice. 'I'm afraid he's in great danger. In your absence, it appears he made his way to the Elliot Jackson Institute. Unfortunately, he was detected. I regret to say he's being held captive by Elliot Jackson.'

11: The Man Who Sold the World

'Stephen, Stephen? Are you safe?' John's thoughts burst into Stephen's mind like water gushing through a broken dam.

Stephen felt a surge of relief. He was sitting on the floor of a tiny office next to Chris, with a burly guard standing over them holding a semi-automatic close to his face.

In normal situations he would have no problem getting away. He could have jaunted to safety or used his powers to unlock the doors. He wouldn't have been able to hurt the guard of course, no Tomorrow Person was capable of inflicting pain or harming anyone. But with Chris here, he was stuck. Not for the first time, he cursed Chris's decision to break into the Institute rather than doing as he'd been told and steering well clear.

'John? What happened? Where are you?' Stephen sent back.

'I haven't got time to explain now. Listen, Stephen, it's vitally important. TIM tells us that you're at the institute. You've got to jaunt out of there. You're in great danger.'

'You're telling me,' Stephen said. He explained concisely what had happened since he'd arrived less than an hour earlier and concluded: 'So the one thing I can't do is jaunt away, or they'll kill Chris. Can't you come and rescue him and bring a spare belt?'

'We simply can't. We've got almost no psionic energy left. It's a struggle just talking to you. There's just no way either of us can jaunt.'

'So, what's the plan? I can't get away, but can you call the police?'

'Well, that's the other thing, Stephen. The stones are beginning to have an impact on people. TIM tells us they're dropping like flies. Thankfully we were able to remove the embryo from your brain before it did any harm. But the whole country is falling apart. The hospitals are overrun, the emergency services are stretched to breaking point and no one seems to be in charge at the government level. It's up to us.'

'Up to me, you mean,' Stephen said.

'Now hang on, you're not totally on your own. We

think we've found a way to stop the nautilus. TIM, take over, I can't keep this up. Good luck.' And John's voice faded.

'The nautilus entity is an extremely dangerous and extremely powerful species,' TIM said. *'The Theta Mindstones are eggs, as you deduced, Stephen – and when a human touching the stone enters a state of deep relaxation, the egg bonds with them and eventually creates an embryo in their brain using the body's own supply of proteins. Once the embryo has been transferred, it grows rapidly. The host has less than a day before the parasite begins to selectively digest the parts of the brain that control human thought, speech and movement – leaving just the more primitive brain functions intact. These creatures effectively take over the host. You were extremely lucky. If we hadn't removed the nautilus embryo from your brain when we did, you would no longer be Stephen, just the husk of his body walking around under the control of a parasitic entity.'*

Stephen felt ill. He touched the back of his head again to feel the wound where the embryo had been extracted.

TIM continued: *'In order to stop the embryos destroying mankind, you need to break the psychic link with their parent.'*

'Yes, TIM. It's in the basement and it's laying eggs like there's no tomorrow.'

'There won't be a tomorrow unless you can stop it. As far as we can ascertain, they have only one weakness. The nautilus stones and embryos are susceptible to negative emotion. We can only assume that the parent will be equally vulnerable. Exploit that weakness, Stephen. Find a way. It's up to you. You have just hours to save the world.'

Before Stephen could reply, Jackson walked in. 'Bring them,' he barked at the guards.

Jackson led them to his office, where he sat down in his leather chair lit by the eerie green light from the giant stone on the central table. Dr Hungerford was standing behind Jackson. Her face was neutral.

Jackson flicked a switch and pop music started to play from the speakers. Stephen recognised the singer as David Bowie.

'I love a bit of Bowie, don't you?' Jackson said, holding his gloved hands together. There was no trace of American or Cockney now. 'You're an interesting young man, aren't you? Not only do you seem to have resisted insemination, you also appear to have some remarkable talents. Who are you exactly? Or more importantly, where are you from?'

'South London.'

'Don't be facetious. Your gifts – the ability to materialise at will. They're not seen on this planet. I'm told they're found elsewhere in the galaxy, yes, but not on Earth. Are you an alien visitor?'

'Elliot.' A voice, high and musical, filled the room. 'Let me chat to the young human.' With each word, the giant stone on the table pulsed more deeply. *So that was where the voice was coming from,* Stephen thought.

'Who was that?' Chris asked.

'That, as you put it, is a she,' said Jackson. 'Stephen has had the honour of seeing her downstairs in the nursery.'

'If she's downstairs, how come I can hear her?'

'You don't have the same qualities as your friend, do you? I wondered, but I suspect you are just a straight. You are just another brainwashed stooge of The Man. Which is a pity. For you.'

'Get me out of this rope and I'll happily show you who's a straight,' Chris growled.

'And once again, the same old violent emotion emerges. This negativity is a disease. These destructive feelings – hate, anger, jealous – they're an obstacle to peace.' Jackson turned to Stephen. 'You've read my book, Stephen. I've been striving all my life for contentment – and here is the answer.

Nautilus. Eternal peace, the likes of which you have never experienced. Before she came to me, I was like you – angry, bewildered, frightened. But under her loving care, I was turned on to the joy of bliss.

'The reason you can share the great privilege of hearing the nautilus is this device.' Jackson waved at the stone. 'It's her interface, the way that I can speak to her and she to me.'

'Elliot, let me speak to the boy.' The voice came from all around them. This time, there was a note of impatience.

'Of course.'

'Doesn't sound like loving care to me,' Chris whispered to Stephen. 'Sounds like he's under her thumb.'

'What if I don't want to talk to your pet Sea Monkey?' Stephen said.

Dr Hungerford stepped forward. 'Stephen, I don't understand. What's happened to you? Why did you break in and try to harm the nautilus? Why are you being so violent?'

'Me being violent? You should ask your little tentacled friend here what she's planning.'

'What's he talking about, Elliot?' Dr Hungerford looked anxious. Stephen studied her face. She doesn't know, he thought. And that could be helpful.

'The boy is talking nonsense,' Jackson said forcefully. 'You know what we're trying to do here – to create a vibe that will bring peace to the world, to end war, to end suffering.'

Mary nodded, but Stephen saw doubt flicker across her eyes.

'To end life, you mean,' Stephen said.

'Okay, that's enough,' Jackson barked. 'You've been honoured with an audience, so speak.'

Stephen considered for a moment, then stepped forward. 'What is it? What do you want?' he asked the nautilus, via the stone.

'How did you do it?' the creature asked.

'Do what?'

The voice was more of a whisper now. If it had been human, Stephen would have said it sounded sorrowful. 'You killed one of my babies. You murdered one. And your friends killed another. How?'

'I don't know what you're talking about.'

'I can smell my baby on you – in your blood and sweat and pheromones. And yet she's not there. There is a void where my child should be. You ripped her out. You destroyed her.'

'Like you're about the destroy the human race!' Negative emotions, John had told him, they were the key to this. But how exactly was Stephen supposed to use them? He was angry and upset himself, but that seemed to have no impact.

Then he remembered the first time he'd used the stone in the Lab. When he'd seen the silverfish and felt repulsion he'd been holding the stone. It had let out a scream, as if it found his disgust unbearable. Maybe that was what was needed here. He needed to touch this giant stone, the interface to the creature in the basement.

Too quickly for Elliot's guards to stop him, he lunged forward and placed both hands on the giant stone. As he did, he summoned every scrap of the rage and frustration and betrayal he felt towards Jackson and pushed it all towards the stone. This man, this hypocrite! Stephen had bought his book; he'd told the others how great he was. Jackson had made him look a fool. Stephen hated him.

And as the anger swelled up, there was a terrific scream of terror and pain around the room. The sound was overwhelming, and Stephen wanted to put his fingers in his ears but he didn't dare to break the link with the stone. He kept his hands flat on its glowing surface. It was pulsing green and white now, and he could feel the heat beneath his fingers.

'Stop him!' Jackson shouted.

Two pairs of hands grabbed Stephen. He tried to shake them off, but they were too strong, and they dragged him away from the stone. He was pushed to the floor, panting, and the scream ebbed away.

'How dare you touch her!' Jackson shouted. 'How dare you!'

The glow of the stone faded back to its more usual, tranquil tone. Stephen had failed this time, but now he knew how he could defeat the nautilus. The only trouble was, first he needed to win over Mary Hungerford.

John had told them that he thought Mary might have latent telepathic powers. Stephen had assumed at the time that John was projecting his own wishes onto the woman. But there had been moments during the tour of the factory, and just now, when Stephen had half heard something. Normally a TP was unable to project their thoughts into the mind of a SAP. But if Mary was a latent telepath..?

Jackson's outburst had certainly come as a shock to her. She was staring at him, as if she was seeing him for the first time.

Stephen concentrated. Jackson was attending to the giant stone, speaking to it soothingly while Dr Hungerford stared at him, a look of growing suspicion on her face. She was vulnerable. There was a chance this could work, but Stephen had to do it now.

'*Mary, Mary, can you hear me?*' he projected towards her with his mind, as forcefully as he could.

Mary started and looked around at Stephen, her eyes wide with shock. He'd done it!

'*Mary, it's me, Stephen. Please don't be scared. I think you've already guessed, but you are special. You can detect people's emotions, can't you. Well, I'm the same, and John is too. Only we can also speak to you and each other, in our minds. Are you okay with that? Do you trust me and John?*'

There was a flicker of a nod.

'*Listen, please. Jackson's lying to you. The eggs – they're harmful. One nearly killed me. This creature isn't helping the human race. It's trying to use us as hosts – to wipe us out. Will you help me – and John?*'

Her eyes widened and her face flushed. She opened her mouth as if to speak, but then seemed to change her mind. She stared at Stephen, and he nodded reassuringly.

'*Listen, Mary, you've heard what the creature just said. This isn't about peace. It's about power.*' He nodded again, and after a second's hesitation, she returned the gesture.

Stephen spoke silently to her again. *'When I give the signal, turn on the microphone – it's in Jackson's drawer.'*

Again, she nodded.

Jackson was standing next to the stone, his face contorted with rage. 'How dare you? How dare you attempt to contaminate the nautilus? You'll pay for this, you pathetic child!'

'I'm not a child,' Stephen said. And at that he reached out to the air surrounding Jackson's body and willed it to rise.

Jackson let out a cry and began to ascend slowly into the air.

The two security guards watched in astonishment, seemingly unable to move. Under Stephen's control, the entrepreneur rose higher until he was six feet off the ground. Then he began to slide sideways in the air until he was hovering over the giant stone, his face facing down.

The pitiful cry of the nautilus filled the room. 'Stop him, stop him!'

Jackson's face was filled with terror as his arms and legs kicked and flung themselves around uselessly. Stephen focused harder, and now Jackson's tie-dye T-shirt began to slide up his body, as if invisible hands were undressing him.

'Sorry, Jackson, but you're a phony,' Stephen said. 'You're a hypocrite and you've sold us out.'

And with that, he let the man fall slowly towards the stone until he was lying prostrate, the bare skin of his arms and belly pressed hard against the surface. The instant that his skin came into contact, a tremendous roar of frustration and pain filled the room. The frustration and anger and fear of Jackson was channelled into the stone and converted into an ear-splitting squeal of emotion.

'Now!' Stephen shouted.

Dr Hungerford reached into the desk drawer and pulled out the microphone. She turned it on and held it over her head. Throughout the factory, the squeal of fear and terror from the giant stone was being broadcast.

'Keep going,' Stephen told her, 'I need to see what's happening.' He gave her a final, reassuring look, then jaunted to the factory floor. As soon as he materialised, he ran to the edge of the hole and peered into the basement below.

This time the room was brightly lit by the glow of white and yellow from the nautilus in the tank. The lights pulsed and shimmied, getting brighter and brighter.

'Stop him! Save me! Save my babies!' The cry of

the nautilus in Jackson's office was broadcast around the factory. And still the squeal grew louder. Stephen could see the creature's tentacles thrashing around, and then a crack appeared in the side of its shell. The thrashing grew wilder and the creature's eyes – no longer blank – were wild with panic.

'*It's a feedback,*' Stephen projected to Mary. '*The creature's own fear is being broadcast back to it. And that's making it worse.*'

And then, with a crashing sound, the shell split and the insides of the nautilus exploded, sending chunks of flesh and green liquid into the sides of the tank which burst open with a terrific release of pressure.

Stephen moved back too late and found himself covered in water and gunge. Abruptly, the screaming stopped and there was silence. Or, at least, near silence. Stephen could hear whimpering through the speakers. He hoped it wasn't Mary.

With one last look at the dead nautilus, he jaunted back to Elliot Jackson's room.

The entrepreneur was standing bewildered and dazed in the cracked and shattered wreckage of the giant egg. 'Man, where am I?' he asked.

12: After All

Mary was waiting in Jackson's office in front of the Mona Lisa, staring intently at the carpet. John watched her from the doorway. *Hello, Mary.* The words weren't said aloud, but she looked up immediately. Her smile melted as she saw his face.

Jackson had been taken away by ambulance, and bewildered fire officers were downstairs touring the factory floor, picking through the gunge, water and shards of glass. Remarkably, no one had been injured in the explosion, although it had triggered the fire alarm. Police were too busy with the chaotic scenes in the rest of the country to attend, and so the factory employees and the resident hippies had been left to themselves.

John was still exhausted from his experience inside TIM, and the jaunt from the Lab had taken all his energy. But he wanted to speak to Mary face to face. He needed to talk to her, to clear the air somehow.

'John, I had no idea, no idea what Elliot, what Jackson, was doing,' Mary said as John walked closer. 'You have to believe me.' Her eyes were pleading, and she clutched her laboratory coat lapel.

'I believe you.' Her face brightened. It was a pretty face, John conceded. He'd known her for weeks, and yet only now had he noticed that. He felt a warm glow as he looked into her eyes, a sense of completeness, excitement and potential. He'd never been in a serious relationship, and yet now he could see a door opening in front of him into a new phase of his life. Perhaps it had taken the shock of his experiences inside TIM to make him aware of his feelings, but he knew now that he felt deeply for her.

And yet. She had betrayed him. Not just him, but all of humanity.

'Why did you trust him, Mary? Wasn't it obvious he was a phoney?' John's question shattered the spell.

Mary stumbled over her words. 'He was a great scientist, John, a visionary. And yes, I was stupid. I see that now. But you must know I never wanted anyone to be harmed. I thought the stones could help humanity reach its potential. I had no idea what they really were.' She paused. And then, 'Can we get over this? Can we be,' she paused again, 'friends.'

And at that moment, John felt a sudden clarity. He knew now what he wanted, and where his priorities lay.

'I'm afraid I don't think that's going to be possible,' he said. 'To be brutally frank, I'm not sure I could ever trust you fully again. Like it or not, you were part of this. And if Jackson had got his way, it would have been the end of humanity. I'm sorry, but I think it's best if we don't see each other again.' And then he walked away.

'But where did this nautilus creature come from – and how did it get to Earth?' Stephen asked sometime later.

They were sitting in the Lab drinking cola.

'There's a million ways,' John said. 'An egg could have been floating through space for generations until it was captured by Earth's gravity. Or it could have slipped through a gap between universes. It may even have been brought here deliberately.'

'Surely no one would be so stupid?' Elizabeth said.

109

'We've made many enemies over the last few years, and not all of them live on Earth,' John reminded her.

Stephen thought of Jedikiah, the evil shape-shifting robot they'd thwarted twice so far. This did seem like the sort of thing he might do.

'The answer to its origins may surprise you,' TIM said, his lights flashing a reassuringly normal colour. 'My chemical analysis of the fragments of shell and tissue that were on Stephen's clothes when he returned from the Institute leads me to conclude that it was not alien at all. In fact, it originated on Earth.'

'What?' John spluttered his drink. 'You're not serious, TIM?'

'I am serious. The isotopic fingerprint of the calcium in its shell suggests that it was born and grew up in the Mariana Trench in the Pacific Ocean many millennia ago.'

'That seems incredible,' Elizabeth said. 'Surely if these creatures lived on Earth, we'd know about it?'

'*Homo sapien* scientists know more about the surface of the Moon than they do about the deepest recesses of the oceans,' TIM told her. 'It is perfectly possible that intelligent life may have evolved independently on this very planet, deep beneath the waters and far out of sight.'

'That's not a reassuring thought,' Stephen said.

Elizabeth shuddered. 'Indeed, it is not. And talking of intelligent life, what happened to your friend, Elliot Jackson?'

Stephen winced at the word 'friend'. 'No friend of mine. Well, by the time the ambulance arrived he was in a bit of a state. He was in some kind of deep trance, unable to speak or move. According to TIM, who sneaked a look at his hospital records, his memory was wiped when the nautilus severed its connection, leaving him in a permanent state of deep relaxation. He has no memory, no ambition and is utterly harmless. The last thing he remembers is living in a commune in the Himalayas.'

'Well, I guess he won't be bothering us again with his plans to wipe out humanity,' John said, chuckling.

The door alarm sounded, and Chris walked in carrying two large paper shopping bags.

'Where have you been?' Stephen asked. 'You set out from the Institute hours ago.'

'It's all right for you Tomorrow People and your jaunting powers, but us Yesterday People have to travel the old-fashioned way by road and parking was a nightmare. But I've bought you a treat. I stopped off at the chippie on the way back from

Hertfordshire, and I've brought you all supper. It's a bit of an East End treat. No need to thank me.'

'Chris, you're a marvel,' John said. 'What did you get?'

'Quadruple chips and enough scallops, scampi and cockles for everyone,' he said triumphantly.

Stephen pulled a face. 'I'm afraid I'll stick with the chips. I think I've had just about enough seafood inside me for one lifetime.'

You may also enjoy…